Moonchee &
Sunbeams

Written by Camille Dalais-Leacher

Illustrations by Glen Holman

Mooncheese & Sunbeams

Written by Camille Dalais-Leacher

Published by

Illustrations and book design by Glen Holman
www.glenholman.com

ISBN: 979-8-8388039-5-5

Mooncheese
& Sunbeams

For my mischievous muses
Milton and Ophelia

Who is the boy on the moon?
Neither you nor I
He sends down stars
Sitting on the moon
Eating chocolate bars
Awake at night
Forever to endure this lonely plight

Who is the girl in the sun?
Shining so hard, beaming her rays
Long, lonely, fiery, frazzling days
Once living on Earth
with her brother, you see
Now locked away without a key

Both alone, but why? You ask
On Earth they had a simple task
Be kind, share, love and remember
Always look after each other forever

Don't fight, don't be cruel,
But instead, if you must,
Discuss, set out rules,
Try to build up your trust

Respect differences
Take it in turn
Those that hear
Are the ones who learn

The boy and girl failed to listen
They fought, they fell,
Their hearts did not glisten

When dark outside,
A blanket of stars
Twinkles so brightly
A powerful glimpse of lessons in life,
To not be taken so lightly

Each little sparkle,
a dusting of guidance:
A word to be kind
A carefree nevermind
A smile to a stranger
A hand held when in danger
An open door to a friend
A please, a thank you, means no end

The girl lights up the day
with her sunny sad smile
She beams across the clouds,
but all the while
Her glow is for her lost brother
Who lies awake, alone in the dark
While she dreams of him
to reignite their spark

The boy meanwhile,
plans his moon cheese getaway
Back to his best friend;
the girl with whom he used to play
He digs with a scrape,
he molds his escape
The stars he invents
are his sister's favourite shape
He sprinkles them with love
and sends them off with kisses
To reach his little sister,
who he every day misses

At last, a rocket built
of moon-dust and rocks
Glued at the seams
with moon-cheese filled socks
He packs his pockets
full of chocolate bars for fuel
He thinks of his best friend
as he prepares to duel

The girl awaits him,
she knows he'll soon be there
For every frazzled star
was sent with care
Knowing now that they
will forever be kind

They will disagree,
of course, but nevermind
They will smile together everyday
Hold hands and laugh when they play
Open doors and be grateful
Enjoy what they have, never be hateful

The boy's fight to the sun
is a fearsome battle
Frosty forces make his
moon-cheese rocket rattle
On he trudges
through starlight and storm
To reach his companion
and rescue the forlorn

A long time later,
the boy arrives by night
The girl is asleep,
so he waits for the light
Not to shock his sister
by being too loud
He whispers: "Jump on"
through a cotton candy cloud
She beams her sunny smile
as soon as she knows
It's her big brother, her best friend,
here to take her home.

Printed in Great Britain
by Amazon